Sales Secrets
From
Your
Customers

By
Barry J. Farber

Sales Secrets
From
Your
Customers

By
Barry J. Farber

CAREER PRESS
3 Tice Road
P.O. Box 687
Franklin Lakes, NJ 07417
1-800-CAREER-1
201-848-0310 (outside U.S.)
FAX: 201-848-1727

SALES SECRETS FROM YOUR CUSTOMERS

ISBN 1-56414-169-1, $8.99

Cover design by A Good Thing, Inc.

Printed in the U.S.A. by Book-mart Press

To order this title by mail, please include price as noted above, $2.50 handling per order, and $1.00 for each book ordered. Send to: Career Press, Inc., 3 Tice Road, P.O. Box 687, Franklin Lakes, NJ 07417.

Or call toll-free 1-800-CAREER-1 (Canada: 201-848-0310) to order using VISA or MasterCard, or for further information on books from Career Press.

Library of Congress Cataloging-in-Publication Data

Farber, Barry J.
    Sales secrets from your customers / by Barry J. Farber.
       p. cm.
    Includes index.
    ISBN 1-56414-169-1 (pbk.)
     1. Selling. 2. Customer relations. I. Title.
    HF5438.25.F3725 1995
658.85--dc20
                                              95-189
                                                CIP

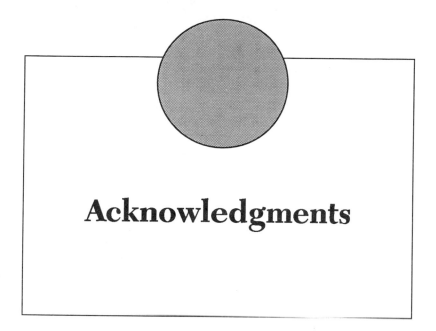

Acknowledgments

Thank you to Richard Farano for supplying the concept for this book.

Special thanks to all the salespeople who gave their time and shared their insights, and especially to all those customers who were so willing to share with me their complaints, praise, thoughts, ideas and opinions. It was a pleasure to listen and learn from you all.

And to Sharyn Kolberg, with great appreciation, for being my valued friend, partner and mind reader.

Special thanks to the Career Press staff: To Ron Fry and Larry Wood for the support and enthusiasm; and to Betsy Sheldon, Ellen Scher, Regina McAloney and Sue Gruber for outstanding quality in production.

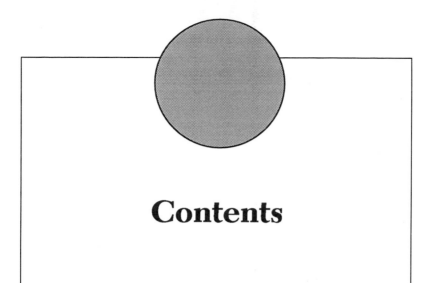

Contents

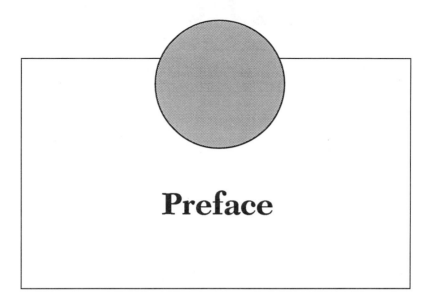

Preface

If you want to know how to be a successful salesperson, there is one person who can give you the answer better than anyone. That person is your customer. Who better to judge your performance, to give you ideas and suggestions, to let you know what you're doing right—and wrong—than your customers themselves? Give them the opportunity to discuss what impresses them about salespeople and where improvements can be made, and they will literally, and eagerly, tell you how to sell.

This book is based on hundreds of interviews conducted with customers to find out what successful salespeople are doing now, and what they could be doing better. But these are not just any customers. They are the customers of the number one sales reps in a variety of industries. They are used to dealing with the best salespeople in the world—

their exceedingly high standards apply to both products and service. Any salespeople who can pass the stringent qualifications these customers present must be at the top of their form.

I did not start conducting these interviews for the purpose of writing a book. In my business as a trainer, one of my main goals is to learn as much as I can about my customer's business. To that end, I like to speak to *their* customers, the ones who deal with the top reps in the company. There are two reasons for this:

1. It teaches me about my customer's industry from the perspective of the people they serve.
2. It gives me feedback to use for my customer; it shows me (and them) how they're doing and what they can do better.

After doing dozens of these interviews, I realized the information I was getting was not industry-specific. It was generic information that could be applied to salespeople in any field. This book will illuminate your thinking about what customers expect from salespeople, based on the kind of service the top reps deliver. It will also remind you of the simple things we sometimes forget, but which are truly important to customers. Some of the quotes and comments that came out of these interviews may seem pretty basic. Many of them appear to be just common sense. However, if hundreds of customers are repeating the same messages about what the best reps do, and what the least successful reps lack, perhaps it's time for all of us to go back and review the basics.

The information in this book, as in the other two books in this series (*Superstar Sales Secrets* and *Superstar Sales Manager's Secrets*), is real-world and results-oriented. It is designed to give any salesperson or manager—neophyte or seasoned professional—models to follow, based on customer evaluations of top reps around the country.

I've been selling for 20 years. I've worked with sales reps, managed them, trained them. I deal with them every day and interview them often. When I listen to these customers talk about their experiences, I realize they spend as much time buying as I do selling and training. What they have to say is guaranteed to stimulate even the most experienced sales professional. They are the true sales experts; listen to them and they will tell you exactly what you need to do to get new accounts, sell more to your present customers and increase your bottom line.

Remember the words of department store founder Marshall Field:

"Those who enter to buy, support me. Those who come to flatter, please me. Those who complain, teach me how I may please others so that more will come. Those only hurt me who are displeased but do not complain. They refuse me permission to correct my errors and thus improve my service."

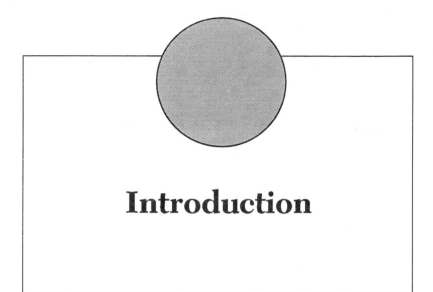

Introduction

What is a customer?

A customer is everyone you come in contact with. You never know who your next customer might be. Obviously, the people you call upon, people who buy your product or service outright, are customers. But then there are friends you run into unexpectedly ("Hey John, I was just thinking about you. I really need a new widget..."), your family, your professional acquaintances. Everyone you come in contact with has contacts. It makes sense to treat everyone you meet with the utmost respect and courtesy, because they just might be your next customer.

Remember, you are a customer, too. You make purchases large and small—groceries, furniture, cars, homes, hardware, software, shoes. Every time you shop, look around. Look at the people selling to you. What are they doing right and wrong? How are you being treated? If you could give this salesperson advice, what would you say?

What do buyers think about salespeople?

On pages 16-17, you will find the results of a poll taken of 100 buyers from the National Association of Purchasing Managers. The buyers were asked two simple questions: "What do you consider most helpful in salespeople?" and "What do you find most objectionable in salespeople?"

We all buy things; it's part of living. The people who participated in this poll buy things for a living. They are professional customers, so to speak. We can assume, therefore, that their advice and insights, based on their combined years of experience, reflect the way most customers feel.

When I read this poll it struck me that these were the very things I had been hearing while interviewing customers over the years. Apparently, there are universal factors that make some salespeople successful, as well as equally universal factors that contribute to others' lack of success.

This is, in fact, the case, as you will see in the pages following the buyers poll. As you consider each of the 10 factors that customers find most valuable and most objectionable, you'll find comments taken from interviews I conducted with hundreds of customers around the country— customers who have dealt with top reps in a variety of industries. Unfortunately, it's impossible to include all the valuable quotes I've obtained from these customers. Therefore, following the customers' quotes, you'll find key points I've culled from the hundreds of others too numerous to print in this book.

Much of what these customers say is the same thing spoken in the varying languages of the industries in which they work. What that means is that there are fundamental rights and wrongs, do's and don'ts that the most successful reps already follow, and those who want to be successful should learn to follow.

What all the customers are really saying is this: Find out what my business is. Then tell me how your product or service can help me run my business better. The goal of many unsuccessful sales reps is to sell their product—to absorb their product's features, functions and benefits, then spit them back into the customer's lap and expect him to be happy about it. They have no time or desire to learn about their customer as a person, or about the customer's business.

Successful salespeople have a different mind-set. They don't sell products. They sell stepping-stones to other people's success. Whether they sell office products, ad space, cable wire, floor coverings, consulting services, photographic supplies—whatever it is—their only purpose in selling that product is to help someone else achieve their goals. If, in helping them achieve their goals, these salespeople also make money, so much the better. This is not just some pie-in-the-sky feel-good philosophy, because what these successful reps know, and what you will discover by taking the advice of the customers interviewed for this book, is that the more you do to help other people achieve their goals, the more money you will make for yourself and for your company. And that's the bottom line.

The following chart is taken from a poll of more than 100 buyers from the National Association of Purchasing Managers. It was originally printed in the newsletter, *Better Repping* by Jack Berman, Encino, California.

What buyers consider most helpful in salespeople	What buyers find most objectionable in salespeople
In order of most times mentioned, here are 10 factors buyers state are most valuable to them:	In order of the number of times mentioned, here are 10 factors buyers state are most objectionable to them:
1. Knowledge. They want salespeople who know products and policies thoroughly. They value technical support most highly.	**1. Lack of preparation.** Buyers hate salespeople who waste time by calling without clear purposes, especially on a busy day.
2. Empathy. They want salespeople who are interested in them. They want salespeople who listen and learn about them, their problems and their goals.	**2. Lack of information.** They were vociferous about dealing with salespeople who didn't know their products or lines and couldn't answer simple questions.
3. Good organization. They want salespeople who come prepared and do not waste their time. They strongly prefer salespeople who have written objectives.	**3. Aggressiveness.** They are turned off by "pushy" salespeople who argue and who "care more about their commission than the customer."
4. Promptness. They expect quick replies to requests for information, especially when a problem rears its ugly head.	**4. Undependability.** They cited salespeople who did not return calls promptly, and who were never there when needed.

5. Follow-through. They look for salespeople who will follow through without continuous badgering. This spells personal reliability.

5. Poor follow-through. They were disgusted with calling salespeople several times to get information the salespeople promised.

6. Solutions. They want salespeople to present innovative solutions to problems. They seek responsiveness and creativity.

6. Presumptuousness. Many were offended by salespeople asking for competitors' quotes and putting down the competition.

7. Punctuality. They expect salespeople to keep appointments promptly, and to let them know if they will be late. They'll excuse tardiness occasionally, not frequently.

7. "Walk-ins." They listed people who called without appointments, with no specific purpose, and they also felt invaded by some telemarketers.

8. Hard work. They appreciate salespeople who work hard. They are impressed by salespeople who put in long and hard hours.

8. "Gabbers." They dislike compulsive talkers. They described the "Gift of Gab" as boring. They were tired of hearing the "latest jokes."

9. Energy. They are impressed by a positive attitude, enthusiasm, affability, consistency and flexibility.

9. Problem avoiders. Salespeople who go to pieces in a crisis, those with no clout and who are afraid of their principles.

10. Honesty. They want specifics instead of generalities. They look for personal integrity.

10. Lack of personal respect. They resent people who go to other people in the company without their knowledge.

17

Chapter 1

Buyers consider most helpful in salespeople...

Knowledge

Customers want salespeople with a broad range of knowledge. They expect you to know your product and policies thoroughly, but they also expect you to know their business, their customers and their competition.

Customer interview: *"Sales reps have to know what they're talking about. And it has to be the right kind of knowledge that I'm looking for—like how many people I reach and who my key customers are. Sometimes reps come on very strong and expound on things like they know it all, like they have all the answers. That's not knowledge, that's just showing off."*

Customer interview: *"To me, a great sales rep is someone who understands my industry, who understands the positioning of my company and who understands our target market. Somebody who can explain the product without* *going through a hundred pages of studies and charts and graphs. I don't have the time—or the necessity—to understand all these things. But I do need to understand how it's going to work for me."*

Customer interview: *"We bought from this company because of the people and their professionalism. Their knowledge of our business was the real difference. I think after you've asked a few questions, you know whether or not the people you're talking to are knowledgeable about your industry. With this company, it's very obvious the people know what they're talking about."*

Key points from customer interviews

- **What you need to know.** Knowledge is a very broad category; the best sales reps are knowledgeable in a variety of areas. They know about their own product, company and industry, and they have detailed knowledge of their customers' companies and industries. They also know the competition, both their strengths and weaknesses.

- **Gaining added value.** The more knowledge you possess, the easier it is for you to come up with solutions to your customers' problems. And that is what gives a rep added value. When you can find solutions that help your customer run his business better, the customer will see you as an employee of his company, not as an outside sales rep.

- **Understanding business concepts.** JoAnna Brandi, president of Integrated Marketing Systems, Inc., in New York and author of *Winning by the Numbers,* says that salespeople need to be more competent in the broad strokes of business.

"I expect a salesperson to understand how my whole business works, not just the piece of it for which he's trying to sell me his widget," she says. "That's how solutions are created, because if you know of problems or challenges in any area of your customer's business, you may be able to help even if it doesn't have to do with your product or service." Brandi feels it's important for salespeople to read and to be well-versed in the liberal arts. "Start reading literature about how people successfully run business, how people successfully market products. That way, when you go to see a client, you're a much bigger resource. You become a consultant on how to run their business better."

Knowledge action steps

⊗ *Study your product inside and out.* Go to the technicians in your company to help you if your product is technically complex. Ask them to explain to you how your product works so that you're not just selling memorized features and benefits. If you know how the product actually works, you'll have a better understanding of how your product can solve customers' problems, and you'll be able to offer them a variety of solutions.

⊗ *Read industry newsletters.* Industry newsletters not only give you industry updates and information, they're also a good source of knowledge about the competition. Keeping up with your competition can keep you one step ahead of them. Also read newsletters and trade publications of your key customers' industries. If you keep ahead of changes in their industry, you may be able to offer solutions to problems before they even arise.

✪ *Speak to successful sales reps.* Experience is usually the best teacher. If your own experience is lacking, borrow from someone else's. Find a mentor in your field and learn as much as you can from him or her.

✪ *Put in extra effort.* If you're selling a tangible product, come in early and actually work with the product so that you know all its kinks and good points. If you sell an intangible, read everything you can get your hands on.

✪ *Talk to customers who have used the product for a while.* There's no greater source of information than an actual end-user. They can give you input about what they like, what they dislike and what's important to them about your product or service. These customers can give you invaluable information about your product. They can also give you ideas of how to use the benefits they've received to sell your product to other customers.

✪ *Learn about the competition.* Study your company's competitive information chart (a chart or book in which reps can record your product's unique selling points, how they compare and contrast to the competition's, and which reps are winning or losing accounts to which competitors. For more information on competitive information charts, see *Superstar Sales Manager's Secrets*). Call your competitors' companies and ask for brochures and information about their products or services. People in your company who have come from other industries may have used competitors' products—or even sold them. Ask them for input and information. And finally, talk to competitive sales reps. There may be times when you can share information, or even exchange leads.

23

Empathy

Customers want salespeople who are sincerely interested in them and their business. They don't want to feel like just another stop on the sales rep's route. They want to know that the rep understands and appreciates their unique goals and challenges.

Customer interview: *"The one thing that is most wasteful of my time is when a salesperson comes in and gives me a canned, generic pitch. I want a program that's going to help with my particular needs and help me solve my problems or be more effective in solving the problems of my customers. It's really important that these people have a good idea of what some of my needs are so they can tailor their presentation directly to me.... I hate it when a salesperson comes in and treats me just like every client* *he or she has done business with before. Every client is different. Although the problems in the industry may be similar, each company has its own set of problems."*

Listening to customers must become everyone's business. With most competitors moving ever faster, the race will go to those who listen and respond most intently.

Tom Peters, *Thriving on Chaos*

Customer interview: *"The best rep understands my objectives and my needs. He knows and is familiar with what I'm interested in and what I want to do, as opposed to making things up just to sell me something—someone who's going to sell me something I need, and understands why I need it."*

Customer interview: *"A good sales rep has my best interest at heart. She understands my business. She should ask questions so that she can understand my objectives. She might even help me define those objectives, and then make a presentation about how my objectives can be met with her product or service."*

Key points from customer interviews

- **Shift your focus.** Empathy means putting yourself in someone else's shoes, understanding their needs, problems and goals. It means helping them find ways to fulfill those needs, to solve those problems and to achieve those goals. There is a quote that salespeople hear often, but don't always heed: "You can get anything you want in this life if you help enough other people get what they want." As salespeople, we're often focused on our commission, on our product, on our sales and on ourselves. We're taking all the focus off the customer and putting it on "me, me, me."

• **Work on listening skills.** Customers tell us over and over again, they buy from reps who listen and respond. You can't be listening if you're doing all the talking. You should be listening 60 to 80 percent of the time. Ask questions to uncover your customer's key needs. Learn about your customer's business. Learn about him personally. What are his interests other than business? Creating rapport is the first step to creating empathy.

• **Make customers feel important.** Studies have shown that recognition is the number one motivating factor for human beings. There is no one more important to your business than your customer; make him feel important, let him know how valued he is. As one customer said, "I like a sales rep to give you the confidence, through their tone of voice and through their actions, that they're on your team and they're working for you all the time, even though in reality you know they're not. Obviously, I'm not that rep's only customer. But when you get the feeling you are their only customer, and that they'll take care of your needs immediately, then you really feel that person's on your side." Concentrate on customers' problems and customers' goals. One of the best questions you can ask your customer is, "What is your greatest challenge in this business?" You want to find out how you can help him face that challenge.

- **Understand your customers' pressure and stress.** JoAnna Brandi says she sees too many salespeople who suffer from EDS: Empathy Deficiency Syndrome. That means they haven't got the vaguest idea of how to be empathetic to people. "Successful salespeople can sometimes be a tad arrogant. They want someone to make a decision and they don't always understand the pressure that person is under. They may not even be the ultimate decision-maker. Technically, the salesperson is supposed to find that out, but sometimes the boss won't get involved, won't even see the salesperson. In that case, you have to play a very empathic, supportive role and help your contact sell your product to his boss."

Empathy action steps

○ *Ask questions that will help you understand the other person's position.* The more you know about your customer's desires and challenges, the easier it is for you to slip into their shoes.

○ *Listen enthusiastically.* Everyone is interesting if you give them a chance. Try to find something about the customer's situation that can generate genuine excitement in you. There's no greater feeling than discovering a way your product or service can solve a customer's problem, so be alert for ways you and your customer can form a relationship.

✪ *Focus on ways to make others feel important.* Often, just giving someone your undivided attention will make them feel important. Let customers know you've heard what they're saying; repeat important points back to them. Concentrate on discovering what concerns them most at this moment, and then let them know you understand those concerns and that you'll do your best to help alleviate them.

Good organization

To put it simply, customers are busy. They don't have time to waste with salespeople who are not prepared with the proper materials and information.

Customer interview: *"I want a sales rep to be set up in advance. He should have all his materials with him and be able to pull out information quickly. They should have ideas and objectives written down so that they could go down the list and make sure they're accomplishing what they came here to do."*

Customer interview: *"I want a sales rep who calls first, and who has something planned out for the meeting. Sometimes they call and say, 'I'm going to be in town next week,' and then they show up and they have nothing in mind for the call. That's a waste of my time."*

Customer interview: *"Sometimes reps come in here and they'll spend more time schmoozing than asking for an order. They talk about everything but how they can do business. The best rep I know calls on us and doesn't waste a lot of time. Whatever his business is, he goes through it pretty rapidly. He gets right to the point. His old-school sales training has taught him how to ask for the order. Some of the salespeople today don't know how to do that. I think that's important."*

Key points from customer interviews

- **Evaluate your customer's style.** Part of being organized is knowing which customers like to spend a few minutes warming up, and which customers like to get right down to business. In New York, a few minutes of rapport building and chitchat is usually enough. By that time, the customer is thinking, "Why is he here? What does he want to find out? What am I going to win from this meeting?" In other parts of the country, people are more comfortable with 10 or 15 minutes of "visiting" before they get down to business. They have to feel they can trust you before they do business with you. You have to feel your customers out, evaluate their personal and corporate styles in order to know how best to proceed.

- **Organize your materials.** Organization is so important that one company I know of actually spends half a day training new salespeople on how to organize their briefcase. It may seem like a trivial point, but think about it. Suppose a customer asks you for some pricing information. You open your briefcase to check the figures and the thing pops up like a jack-in-the-box, papers flying all over the place. What does this customer think? He probably thinks, "If this rep is so unorganized in my office, how is he going to take care of my complicated needs?"

There are accordion files you can get in any office supply store that can help you organize the various materials and forms you carry around with you. Or you can put together a presentation kit in a three-ring binder with tabbed sections. You could include a section on the product itself, a section on product accessories, a section for information about your company and a section for testimonial letters (see "Customer Portfolio" information in *Superstar Sales Secrets*). The more organized you are, the more confident you can be and the better you can concentrate on the customer's needs. It's difficult to think of solutions to your customer's problems when you're busy thinking, "Now where did I put that information sheet?"

- **Organize your presentations.** Your presentations should be organized as well as your materials. Follow the Four T's of Presentations:

  1. *Tell them what you're going to tell them.* Let your customers know what you're going to talk about and why it's going to be important to them. You might open your presentation with a statement like, "What I'm going to do is take you through our new product line and demonstrate exactly how we can help you decrease production time."

  2. *Tell them.* Go through your presentation, following the outline you proposed above.

3. *Test them on what you've told them.* Ask questions that will get you feedback. You want to know: Is the presentation hitting home? Does it make sense? Is it addressing their criteria?

4. *Tell them what you've told them.* Summarize your ideas so that the presentation is focused and complete.

- **Organization during the call.** Another important area of organization is taking notes during the call. When you begin the call, you might say, "What I'd like to do today is to find out as much as possible about your needs, to add to what I already know about your company, and I'd like to see if there's an opportunity for us to move forward and for you to gain some of the benefits from our company's services. By the way, do you mind if I take a few notes?" It often makes customers feel comfortable to know that there is a stated structure and objective to the call.

- **Organization after the call.** After the call (if it is part of a longer sales cycle), send the customer a letter restating the three or four most important issues that were discussed during the call. This will show the customer that you are organized and that you were listening carefully. At the end of the letter, include an indication of the next step of the sale (that you'll be calling to set up a demonstration/appointment, etc.).

Organization action steps

✪ *Plan your day the night before.* Each evening, go over your to-do list, or make a new one, so that you know exactly what needs to be done the following day. Wake up doing instead of thinking about what you're going to do.

✪ *Understand your sales cycle.* Have some method of tracking where you are in the sales cycle with each of your customers. This can be done through an organizational chart that tracks activities, through daily reports you hand in or through your own journal of activities. However you keep track, be sure you know who you need to call on, when you need to call them and what you need to prepare for each meeting.

✪ *Pre-call organization.* Ask yourself these three questions before every call:

1. What is the goal of this call?

2. What do I need to find out during this call?

3. What's the next step after this call?

✪ *Let the customer in on the organization of the call.* At the beginning of the call, make a general benefit statement, such as, "Thanks again for taking the time to see me today. Before I tell you about my company's background and achievements, I want to learn more about your situation and see if there's an opportunity for us to move forward." This kind of general statement lets the customer know what you're there for and what they're about to hear. This not only helps you with your own organization, it makes the customer feel as if he's with someone who values his time.

Promptness

Customers want salespeople to return their calls as quickly as possible, whether they're asking for pricing information or calling to complain about poor service.

Customer interview: *"My favorite rep is someone I know I can depend on. Whenever I leave a message for him, he calls me back by the end of the day, or at the latest, first thing the next morning."*

Customer interview: *"I know I can trust my rep. I know she'll take care of me. If I need something right away, I can trust her to take care of me and get it to me as fast as she possibly can."*

Key points from customer interviews

- **Your call can be extremely important to their business.** For the customer, the measure of a good salesperson comes after the product is delivered. You may think that the speed with which you return a customer's call is a minor consideration, but most customers consider it major. Their business could be on the line. Customers need to know that questions they have will be answered promptly and problems will be attended to.

- **Solved problems create loyal customers.** Some salespeople are reluctant to return customers' calls because they're afraid to face problems. However, as has been said many times before, problems are opportunities. If you can help a customer solve a problem, you are really helping yourself and your business. The United States Office of Consumer Affairs has collected information about how consumers handle problems they have with products and services. One of their most interesting findings states that of all consumers who make a complaint about a product or service and receive a satisfactory response, 70 percent become the company's most loyal customers.

- **Why serve customers well?** Jay Goltz, president of Artists' Frame Service in Chicago, the largest custom picture-framing company in the world, feels that taking care of customers goes beyond responding to statistics. "Everybody quotes the statistic, 'One happy customer tells three people and one unhappy customer tells seven.' What did you do before you knew this? Did you say to yourself, 'If they tell seven people, I'd better start taking care of my customers!' How about taking care of the customer because it's the right thing to do? Whether they tell one person or 50, it doesn't really matter to me. I want to take care of that one customer because that's what I'm supposed to do."

Promptness action steps

✪ *Return all calls as soon as you can, even if you know they're concerning a problem.* A customer will respect any effort you make to help. They will not respect you, knowing you're afraid to call them back. The best way to lose business is to let a problem go unattended.

✪ *Make sure you have a number of ways for people to get in touch with you.* Here are some options. Have a beeper so that people can reach you at all times. Have a separate line (with answering machine) installed at home so that customers can reach you during off-hour emergencies. Leave a message on your voice mail that tells callers when and where you can be reached.

✪ *Keep your promises.* If you tell a customer you'll fax figures by the end of the day, or send information overnight, do it. If you're not sure you can get the information that fast, tell the customer how long you think it might take and then surprise them by getting it done sooner.

Follow-through

Customers want salespeople to keep their promises. They don't want to be badgered, but they want to know they won't be forgotten after the sale has gone through.

Customer interview: *"I think the best thing a salesperson can do is follow up with his customer. Once a salesperson has made a sale, if he doesn't follow through— at least call the customer and say, 'Are you satisfied?' or 'Is there anything more we can do?'—the customer feels stranded, abandoned."*

Customer interview: *"Sometimes, once a company has my business, they tend to take it for granted and sit back on their laurels. This is what I'd like to see: After every single order is executed, the salesperson should hold some sort of post-sale meeting with me. That's important* *to make sure that all of our objectives were met, and also to find out if there were any things that occurred during the course of that sale that can be improved upon. I want to know that you'll take care of these problems, that they'll be addressed before we do any further business."*

Anyone can make a one-time sale. It's the follow-through that keeps the customer coming back for more.

Customer interview: *"The thing that turns me off about salespeople is when they hound me, when they call month after month just to bug me. The people I buy from are the ones who have good information. They don't call me every week with something, but when they do it's legitimate. They say, 'Here's an idea that might help you' and they're right. I know they understand my business by the information I get from them. Sales reps who do their homework and are educated will do much better than those who are just trying to push something down my throat."*

Key points from customer interviews

- **Have a purpose for every call.** One of the most frequent comments customers make is how they don't like to be pestered by salespeople. But that doesn't mean they don't want you to stay in touch. They want to know that you have a purpose for calling other than to ask, "Are you ready to do business again?"

- **Develop a system to keep track of contacts.** It's helpful to have some kind of system to aid you in keeping track of which accounts you've sold and when to call them back. I use a wall board, where I've tacked up my customers' names and can see right in front of me the last time I did a program for them, sold them a product or called them on the phone. Then I can determine the appropriate time frame in which to call them again. Keeping their names in front of me also helps me think about what I can do for them or share with them that would help make a difference in their business or personal lives.

- **Find new ways to "reach out and touch" your customers.** JoAnna Brandi says that there is a direct link between the number of times you contact the customer and the number of times the customer buys. But you have to be able to judge the fine line between keeping in touch and being annoying. "A lot of people want the attention from their salespeople, but they don't want to be called a lot. So I recommend that salespeople find a variety of ways to touch their customers." There's a new term Brandi reports hearing called "customer portals."

  "The trick for salespeople is to find as many customer portals as possible—as many ways as possible to contact the client without being intrusive. Use the mail, use the fax, use the Internet. You can even occasionally leave a quick voice-mail message when you know the client is out. I've called customers and left a message that said, 'I was just thinking about you. I know you're a runner and I thought you'd be interested to know that there's a program on running on TV tonight.' "

- **Reinforce your customer's decision to buy.** Another tip that Brandi has about follow-through has to do with reinforcing the customer's decision to buy, especially if it's a first-time sale. "Customers want to know they made the right decision," she says. "And they want to know that when they go to the boss, that boss will say they made the right decision." Her solution? Ward off buyers' remorse by sending customers another customer's success story, or send them an article that shows how others in their industry are successfully using your product or service.

- **Don't forget the human touch.** Tony Parinello, author of *Selling to VITO (Very Important Top Officers)*, adds one note of caution to these alternative methods of contact, however. He feels that many salespeople are relying too much on technology and not enough on face-to-face, handshake-to-handshake follow-up. "You've got to make yourself available to the VITOs on a regular basis. You can't rely on technology to do it for you. There's no replacement for that handshake once a month or every other month, letting them know you're working to help them meet and achieve their goals."

Follow-through action steps

✪ *Follow up after every single order.* Find out if your product or service is meeting expectations and if there's anything else the customer might need.

✪ *Establish a schedule for follow-up calls and customer visits.* Ask the customer about his or her expectations of a salesperson after a sale. Find out how often they would like you to call—once a week, once a month, once a quarter, etc. Write call-back dates in your calendar so you won't forget.

✪ *Write thank you letters for appointments, demonstrations, orders, referrals, etc.* Just a short, handwritten note can make the difference between a one-time sale and a committed customer. This is an easy task which can be done at home in a short period of time, yet not many salespeople take the time to do it. This is a surefire way of standing out from the rest of the crowd.

Solutions

Customers want salespeople to realize they are not just selling products or services—they're selling solutions to problems. Customers appreciate salespeople who are creative and innovative, and who can think "outside the box."

Customer interview: *"The best sales rep I know is a woman who's become a resource for me in a variety of areas. I use her on a consultative basis, almost. She helps me evaluate opportunities. Not only with her product— she's a constant fountain of information in trying to find different ways to portray my point of view to the market. I never get the feeling that she's just selling me something; she's interested in my success."*

Customer interview: *"Our company feels that we are partners with our customers. The better we work as partners, the longer-term we're going to do business and the more business we're going to do. If a salesperson approaches me in that fashion, I can be a very loyal guy. I know I can use a rep as a consultant when I'm sitting across the desk from him and I ask him a question, and I don't get chapter and verse about his product—I get chapter and verse on what's in my best interest based on his experience in the marketplace."*

Customer interview: *"I need a rep who understands what my concerns are and what I'm trying to get at. A really good rep can actually help you understand what you're looking for. People who run businesses don't always know where their market is. A good rep can actually say, 'How about going in this direction?' They see a lot of different businesses in my industry. They might have a better understanding than I do of what motivates my customers to buy. I need them to help me understand these things."*

Customer interview: *"With some reps, it's obvious that they're only interested in the dollar amount of the sale. They're not interested in trying to promote your business. A good rep approaches the sale from what you need to get your business going. They'll often help you by showing you examples of what other people have done to be successful. They're not after the quick sale, they want a long-term relationship. They help you come up with ideas that are outside of their product or service. Unfortunately, with most reps you get the feeling they're more self-serving that customer-serving."*

Key points from customer interviews

- **Create customer partnerships.** There's a saying that, if customers were just buying price and product, we could just hire brochures as salespeople and send them out. One of the most valuable assets a salesperson has is the ability to create partnerships with their customers. That means keeping the customers' overall business goals in mind and helping them find new resources whenever necessary. It may mean recommending a competitor on occasion if your company or product can't do the job. It means knowing your product so well that you know every conceivable application and adaptation possible. It means using your imagination in combination with your knowledge and experience to come up with ways to improve your customers' bottom line (and thereby improve your own).

- **Create added value.** When I'm setting up a sales training program for a company, I usually have contact with several different people in the organization. At one of my accounts, I had the opportunity to talk to the person who books the seminars for this company. Her job is to find space for the seminars, book hotels, arrange transportation, etc. I remember I once spent an hour on the phone with her teaching her how to negotiate with hotels to get better room rates. This was helpful to her, because when it came time for review she could show her supervisor documented evidence of how she saved the company thousands of dollars; it was good for the company because of the decrease in their expenses; and it was good for me because she told her supervisors what I had done which then provided added value beyond the training.

- **Exceed your customers' expectations.** Tony Parinello recommends that salespeople help their customers in three areas:

  1. Salespeople should offer ideas on how to help the customer drive revenues.

  2. Salespeople should offer ideas on how the customer can maintain their customer base. If you have some ideas on how to help this customer hold on to their hard-earned market share, you're going to earn your right to stay there.

  3. Salespeople should offer ideas on how to add on business from their existing customers.

  "As a sales rep," says Parinello, "you need to be able to out-deliver, out-perform and exceed your customers' expectations in these three basic areas."

Solutions action steps

✪ *Dive in with enthusiasm and effort.* Dive into your own products and services and what they have to offer. With equal energy, explore the customer's business so that between the two you can come up with innovative, exciting solutions that will benefit your company and his.

✪ *Keep your mind open.* "The way things have always been done" may not be the best way to solve your customers' problems. Instead of saying, "It can't be done," ask yourself, "Why not?"

✪ *Ask yourself "What resources do I have available to influence the customer's bottom line?"* Start thinking outside the confines of your own product or service. Who do you know who might be able to help? How can you put the customer in touch with another vendor who might have a solution—even if it's the competition? What would be the ideal solution to this problem, and how close can you come to making that happen?

Punctuality

This is one of those comments that seems so basic...but customers need to feel that their time is as important to you as it is to them. They understand delays in schedule, as long as you let them know you will be late.

Customer interview: *"I know salespeople can't always help being late. But my time is precious. If they're on the road and there's no phone in the car, stop and call or have someone in your office call me. If the rep can't even keep his own schedule straight, it makes me think he won't be able to keep delivery schedules either."*

Key point from customer interviews

- **Show respect and common courtesy.** This is based on common sense. Salespeople should keep

Vince Lombardi time: He set his watch 15 minutes fast. That way, if he was five minutes late according to his watch, he was still 10 minutes early. It sounds so basic to remind salespeople to call if they're going to be late, but a lot of people don't. Sometimes reps are afraid to call when they're running late, because they think the customer will use that as an excuse to cancel. That may happen occasionally, but it's more likely that your call will reinforce your trustworthiness and concern for the customer's time.

Punctuality action steps

○ *Make telephone appointments.* Tell the customer you'll call at 10:10 or 10:15, and then keep to your schedule.

○ *Plan next week this week.* The time you spend on the phone today should result in scheduling appointments for next week or next month. This not only keeps you punctual, it gives you something to look forward to. There's nothing better to keep you energized than to know you've got a week of appointments—and opportunities—ahead of you.

○ *Prioritize your activities so that what must get done does get done.* Some activities are more urgent than others. List your activities in order of importance; that way if some less important things don't get done today, they can be shifted to another day without affecting your sales productivity.

Hard work

Customers appreciate salespeople who put in long and hard hours, even occasional weekends. They want to know that they will get a 110 percent effort from a rep who cares about them and their business.

Customer interview: *"If I was a salesperson, I'd do things the reps I know never do. I'd come in here with a cleaner every once in a while and clean off the samples. Would it be so difficult to come in with a rag and a bottle of Windex? If I didn't want to do it, I'd hire a young kid for $5 an hour to do it. But I'd see that my products were clean and cared for. Most salespeople don't want to make the effort."*

Customer interview: *"We're not a company that looks solely for price. What's more important to us is the extra* *effort and degree of service we get from the rep and from the company. There's one sales rep who's outstanding in both effort and service. If we need a product or an answer to a question, she's right there with it. If we have an unexpected workload that exceeds our supply, she's willing to go out and make courtesy calls on other customers to borrow the product to get us through the crunch period. We had a case where she even drove the product down from Greensboro to Charlotte that day. Because of her, we would not change vendors for a difference in price."*

Key points from customer interviews

- **The road to success is paved with hard work.** When we look at successful people, we usually see the results of their blood, sweat and tears. We don't see the hard work and extra effort that went before. High achievers in any field are willing to give their all to everything they do in order to see their goals become reality.

- **Activity is the antidote to depression.** Salespeople often get depressed by the amount of rejection they face every day on the job. However, usually this depression is caused by lack of activity. As soon as you renew your efforts at making contacts, pursuing leads and establishing follow-up procedures, the depression begins to lift and productivity begins to climb. When we put in the effort, we know that further along the road there will be a payoff.

- **Extra effort builds credibility.** The best sales reps start work early and stay late. If you make cold calls at 6 p.m., you often find the business owner or top officer working late as well, and you also find that they respect the fact that you're working late. I know sales reps who have installed equipment on weekends so that they wouldn't interfere with their customer's business. The customer was so appreciative of the rep's hard work that he bought several more products, worth thousands more dollars, from that rep.

Hard work action steps

✪ *Try the "do one more" principle.* Whenever things start getting tough or an obstacle appears, there is one thing you can do that doesn't take any kind of special talent, and that is, work a little bit harder. Stay one extra hour. Make one more phone call. Write one more thank-you note. Do just one more activity than you think you can. Customers will sense that extra effort and it will pay off in the end.

✪ *After every task, ask yourself, "Can I do it better?"* Do all the little extras you'd rather not do. There's one thing everyone has in common: There's always room for improvement.

✪ *For the next 30 days, put 110 percent into everything you do.* Whether it's taking out the garbage or presenting to the biggest account in your territory, put everything you've got into all your activities. At the end of the 30 days, look back and see what a difference it made in all aspects of your life.

Energy

Energy, enthusiasm and a positive attitude can go a long way in forging long-lasting customer relationships.

Customer interview: *"A salesperson needs to stimulate me into buying his products. He needs to come in with some energy, some enthusiasm, some pizzazz."*

Customer interview: *"My favorite rep is a woman who is incredibly energetic and enthusiastic. She's funny. She doesn't just understand my needs and my business, she understands me as a person, she understands my culture. She does her job really well and she makes me feel good at the same time."*

Key points from customer interviews

- **Energy is the key.** When I interviewed William Clements, former governor of Texas, for my book

Diamond in the Rough, he told me, "Energy is the secret to everything. You can be a person of great integrity, character and all these other wonderful things, but if you don't have the energy, and if you don't really put your shoulder to the wheel, so to speak, and start pushin', you're not going to get to first base."

• **Pro-active versus reactive.** When you look at high achievers in any field, the first thing you will notice is their high energy. They are pro-active personalities; they make things happen instead of sitting back and waiting for things to happen to them. They have a positive attitude—based on a belief in themselves and their abilities—which keeps them going even when they encounter rejection and setbacks.

• **Enthusiasm and a belief in what you're doing are the foundations for success.** Successful sales reps are enthusiastic about their job, about their product or service, and about their company. Enthusiasm comes from the Greek word "entheos" which means "the god within." Enthusiasm is a zeal for living that gives us energy and drives us forward. Enthusiasm can often carry us far beyond any skill or talent we may be lacking. And enthusiasm is contagious. When you call on a customer with energy and enthusiasm, it means that you believe in your product or service, and are excited about what you have to offer your customer. This isn't a false performance; sincere positive attitude and belief in yourself and your product cannot be faked.

Energy action steps

○ *Concentrate on the positive.* Sometimes we get so bogged down by the things that are "wrong" in our lives that we forget to be grateful for the things we have. Every so often, take a step back and look at everything you've achieved so far. Celebrate how far you've come, without worrying about how much there is still to do.

○ *Assess your physical activity level.* Physical activity—whether it's a sport, a workout at the gym or a brisk walk around the block—revitalizes and regenerates us in body and mind.

Honesty

This is a customer's number one demand: Be honest with me. Over and over again customers say they want to know up front if there are problems with products or delivery. They'd do repeat business with a vendor who told them about a delivery delay beforehand, but they'd never do business again with a salesperson who lied or tried to cover up an existing problem.

Customer interview: *"Sometimes when I order a product or service from a company, they can't make a delivery, through no fault of their own. Tell me about it. If a shipment comes in two or three days late, tell me about it. Tell me if my expectations are too high. Tell me if the* *price I want is impossible for you. If I want to pay a dollar for something that costs you $1.25, tell me, 'My cost is higher than that, and I need this much markup to be able to provide you with the service you need.' Tell me if you cannot make a commitment you previously made. If you can't be honest with me, why call on me?"*

Key points from customer interviews

- **It only takes one little lie...** A few years ago, one of my customers told me a story. She had an insurance rep who had sold her insurance for 16 years, a rep she liked and respected. Then, the rep made a fatal mistake. He tried to sell my customer a policy she clearly didn't need. It was obvious the rep was pushing the policy so he could collect his commission. That one meeting ruined 16 years of a relationship. My customer never did business with him again. It took all those years to build a strong relationship and one second to lose it. One moment of dishonesty.

- **There is no excuse for dishonesty.** Any customer would much prefer to be told about a problem so that you and he can begin to think about solutions. Customers appreciate a sales rep who is straightforward, who lays his cards out on the table. A good salesperson lays out all the details up front so that there are no questions later about hidden charges. Some reps are afraid to show added charges and hope that the customer won't notice them on the invoice. But most customers do notice, and many a prospective sale has been lost because a rep tried to put something over on a customer.

● **Customers want an honest, one-on-one relationship.** "Customers know that salespeople make a commission based on the sale of their product or service," says Alex Nicholas, president of Applied Concepts Inc., a Florida-based sales and management consultant and trainer, "so things are slightly skewed to start off. But customers also want to buy. They want salespeople to communicate with them honestly, to be frank in their discussions of what their product or service can do for them. They want someone who can appreciate their unique situation and their unique problems. Customers are not naive, but they do want to feel that the salesperson is making a special effort to understand their situation."

Honesty action steps

✪ *Seek truth in everything you do.* What is the core truth, the underlying benefits of your product or service? How does it apply in each selling situation?

✪ *Seek truth in others.* Look for the best in everyone. Look for the common bond on which you can build a relationship.

✪ *Value your integrity.* Stand behind your beliefs. If you lack belief in what you're selling, dig deeper and make discoveries about your product or service that will shore up that belief. If you can't find anything, move on. You can never find meaningful achievement doing something in which you don't believe 100 percent. You may find temporary success, but it won't last. True success is based on a foundation of honest passion for your work.

Sell yourself, as well

Since what most customers are really buying is a personal relationship with their sales reps, the following idea will help you promote the added value and uniqueness of you a salesperson.

When you go out on a sales call, you always carry brochures about your company and your product and service with you. That's because customers want to know what they're getting; they want to be able to study the background and benefits of something they're about to purchase. However, studies have shown that 95 percent of a sale is made because the customer buys the individual salesperson, not the product or service.

So why not provide your customers with a one-page brochure about you? You could begin by letting your customers know how long you've been in the business. If you're just starting out, lead off your biography with a mission statement such as, "My goal as a sales rep is to serve my customers with 110 percent effort to satisfy their needs, not only during the sale but long after, as well. I promise to answer their questions honestly and respond to any concerns as quickly as possible."

Include any awards you may have gotten from your company, and add a few short testimonials from satisfied clients. You can end the brochure by saying, "The purpose of this short biography was to let you know that in our business you're not just buying our product, you're buying a person, as well. I'm that person, and I want you to get to know me and to know that you can count on me for the kind of quality service you expect."

Chapter 2

Buyers find most objectionable in salespeople...

Lack of preparation

Customers don't like salespeople who call them on the phone or come by without a specific purpose in mind. Every once in a while, it's okay to say, "I just wanted to keep in touch," but it's better to have a reason for doing so.

Customer interview: *"I do a lot of advertising in newspapers and I get avalanches of calls from small papers who want me to advertise in their paper. They never stop calling. But they never have anything special to say. Every newspaper tells you they have all the statistics on why their particular paper is the one I should advertise in. But it's rare that you come across somebody who is not just mouthing what the company has told them to say."*

Customer interview: *"I think salespeople should have more of a long-term focus. Many vendors try to blitz a* *large company and sell to all areas at once. I think they should go in, find one area of the company where they can really make an impact, and do a flawless job on the first one or two opportunities they get. That's a better idea than making a pest out of yourself before you've earned the right to get business from other parts of the company. We're looking for long-term relationship vendors who get to be considered a member of our internal team. It takes time, dedication and hard work on both sides. Very few clients are going to be willing to do that unless they see that the vendor is prepared for the job you're asking them to do."*

Key points from customer interviews

- **A reason for every call.** Imagine this scenario: A week ago, a buyer agreed to take 15 minutes out of his busy schedule to see a salesperson who has called him several times. On the day of the appointment, the buyer is up to his ears in paperwork, as well as trying to solve a crisis caused by another vendor's shipping snafu. The salesperson walks in and says, "I just wanted to touch base with you and find out if you're ready to buy." Any wonder the buyer is furious?

    There are some salespeople who want to rely on amazing coincidences to make their sales. "If I just call this guy one more time," they think, "he'll finally decide to buy from me." But why should he? What have you got to offer that will answer his most basic question of all, "What's in it for me?" There must be a reason for each and every call you make, and a clearly thought-out benefit to the buyer.

- **Keep service updated.** Having a well-thought-out purpose for your call is necessary whether you're calling on a prospect or a customer you've had for 10 years. Giving long-standing customers the same level of service constantly over 10 years is not always enough. For the first two years, that level of service may have sufficed. But their marketplace may be changing, and you need to learn about and keep questioning what's going on, so you adapt what you're offering to help that customer keep up with changes in his industry. It's not enough just to say "Hi" every once in a while to let them know you're still around—your purpose is always to keep up with what's going on in their business and how they're changing, so you can better help that business thrive and grow.

Lack of information

Customers often depend on sales-people as a source of information on a variety of subjects. They said the worst reps were the ones who lacked specific information about their own products and/or general information about the customer's business.

Customer interview: *"One of the biggest problems I have right now is that there are a lot of new products on the horizon; it's hard to decipher which one is the best one, which one is the best buy. As a buyer, I have to sit down at some point and say, 'Is this really any good? Is it better than XYZ Company's product?' A good sales rep has to know everything there is to know about his product—and about the competition—to be able to tell me how his product stands out from the rest."*

Customer interview: *"There are situations that arise with some vendors where you have to question the input you get from a particular person. I'm not always sure that person knows what he's talking about. For instance, he'll quote me one price and then come back and tell me another. Or he'll say he has a product in stock, and come back the next day and tell me it will be six weeks before it can be delivered. I never know if he's telling me what he thinks I want to hear, or if he just doesn't know what he's talking about."*

Key points from customer interviews

- **Keep your customers educated.** "One thing customers consider most helpful from salespeople is education," says JoAnna Brandi. "And I don't mean handing them a brochure. They want a salesperson who understands the product and the process well enough that they can explain it to the customer in simple terms." The worst thing you can do in a sales situation is try to wing it. Sometimes the best way to build your credibility is to admit that you don't know the answer to your customer's questions. Of course, the next step is to let them know you'll get back to them as soon as possible with the answer—and then follow up immediately. Customers respect a rep who is able to say, "We just got this product on line and I'm not 100 percent sure of its capabilities in that area. Let me find out and get back to you by 10 a.m. tomorrow." When you do get back to them the following morning, they know they can trust the information you're giving them, and they know they can trust you to keep your word.

- **Don't promise anything unless you're 100 percent sure it can be done.** Never assume anything. Suppose a customer says, "I can only purchase this product from you if I can have it delivered, installed and ready for use by Friday morning." Don't automatically say "yes" when you don't know if it can be done. The customer will be moving ahead on his agenda on the basis of your promise. If you find out two days later, it will be disastrous for your customer and for your relationship. Never give out information that is not based 100 percent on what you know to be true.

- **Provide your customers with information of interest to them.** One of the things customers find the most helpful is salespeople who can provide them with education, who send them articles of interest for both their business and personal lives. A buyer wants the type of relationship that shows the salesperson isn't only interested in making a sale, but is also interested in helping that buyer do a better job for his company.

- **Give customers suggestions based on others' successes.** Customers also appreciate it when you have information about their competition. They don't expect you to give away trade secrets, but if you see someone else in their industry doing something successfully, you will do well to pass that information along. One customer said, "A good rep will keep me informed about what my competitors are doing, what people are looking at and looking for when they go into competitors' stores. Am I displaying the materials properly? If I'm not, maybe the rep can give me some tips on how to do it better. That will help his sales and mine."

Aggressiveness

Customers often complained about "pushy" salespeople, ones who argue and try to convince customers to spend more than is necessary. They felt those reps were only interested in their commissions and didn't really care how they got them.

Customer interview: *"In the narrow view, what I do is buy ad space. But I don't view what the salespeople do as selling me space. I hate it when they pitch me in this fashion: If you run six times, it's this price, if you run eight times, it's this price. Don't sell me space like you're selling me groceries. If any salesperson comes in here just quoting me prices in numbers of ad runs, I won't listen to them. Come to me with a proposal. Show me you've put some thought into what you're trying to sell me. Because* *you've got plenty of competition and I can go to plenty of other places. Tell me why I should advertise with you, and what you can do for me. Show me you're interested in my success; don't just show me you're interested in my dollars."*

Customer interview: *"The biggest turnoff is a pushy salesperson. That means they're not willing to listen."*

Customer interview: *"A lot of the reps I run into are incredibly pushy. They want to sell me something without any feedback about what their product can do for me. I find that very disturbing. They don't ask the right questions, like, 'What are you trying to achieve?' 'Who are you trying to reach?' 'What would you like to get out of this relationship?' "*

Key points from customer interviews

- **Aggressiveness versus assertiveness.** The complaint that many salespeople are too "pushy" is the most frequent one I've heard from customers. The number one feedback is that customers don't like aggressiveness. There is a difference between aggressiveness and assertiveness. Aggressiveness means you're being an obnoxious pest and trying to push your product or service on people whether they need it or not. You're assertive when you believe 100 percent in the value of your product, and you want to do your best to see that this customer benefits from what you have to offer.

- **Build trust with your customers.** In other words, it's not the quantity, but the quality of the calls customers complain about. Customers are impressed when salespeople are persistent because they believe that their products or services can benefit the customer. But there are times when it's necessary to back off and rethink your approach. If the customer perceives that you are simply trying to make a sale, they probably won't buy from you. Customers know your job is to sell them something; they don't expect to get something for nothing. But there are many people from whom they can buy; they expect you to tell them why they should buy from you. They want a relationship in which they feel comfortable; they want to be able to trust you.

- **Respect the customer's right to object.** You are aggressive when you violate customers' trust, when you don't respect the customers and their opinions and ideas. Customers don't want to argue with you. Lisa Kanarek, Dallas-based author of *101 Home Office Success Secrets,* says that sales reps need to be patient, to make an effort to understand their customers' objections and be willing to answer customers' questions. "I personally had a situation with a salesperson recently where that didn't happen," says Kanarek. "I got into a yelling match with someone. I will never go back to that business establishment again. If you fight with a customer, you both lose."

- **Review your listening skills.** If you have to argue, you haven't been listening to the customer. If you're really running into resistance in a sale, ask, "Is there something that I've missed that has not really moved us forward?" Use your common sense and empathy to put yourself into your customer's mind-set and try a different approach.

Undependability

Customers cited salespeople who waited for days to return phone calls and who were always difficult to reach.

Customer interview: *"I know some reps, when they're trying to get your business, they call you all the time and they answer your calls right away. But after the sale, they disappear. Suddenly they're never in the office, and you have to leave three or four messages before they call you back. As far as I'm concerned, that's the best way to lose me as a customer."*

Customer interview: *"I don't really understand this, but it happens a lot. They work so hard to get me as a customer, and then when I do buy from them, it's like they don't want to be bothered. They're on to greener pastures. They return my call four days later with no apology or explanation of why it took so long. I treat my customers* *with respect and courtesy, and I expect them to do the same for me."*

Key points from customer interviews

- **Do customers know how to reach you?** The best way to overcome the perception that you are undependable is to follow the action steps under "promptness" and make it easy for customers to get in touch with you. "If customers can't find you," says Lisa Kanarek, "they'll go with someone else." You might even want to give customers items like pens or desk accessories with your name and number printed on them so they'll have easy reference at all times.

- **Organize your method of leaving and receiving messages.** Being able to return calls and stop the phone-tag syndrome is a matter of organization. If you are out on the road all day, be sure to leave enough time between appointments so that you can check back with your office, voice mail or answering machine. If you get a message from a customer and you really don't have time to return the call that day, ask your secretary to call the customer and tell her you're on the road and you'll call tomorrow at 10 a.m. (or whatever time is good for both you and the customer).

Poor follow-through

Customers often said they had to ask for information and answers several times before they got it. They felt let down by sales reps' empty promises.

Customer interview: *"We're looking for long-term vendor relationships. We don't want to have a one-sided relationship after the sale where we always have to call the sales rep to get what we need. I don't expect the rep to take my business for granted. We both have to work hard at keeping it beneficial for both of us. I'll only be disappointed one or two times, then I'll have to go with somebody else who cares more about maintaining a good relationship. The salesperson should do whatever it takes to see that doesn't happen."*

Customer interview: *"When my best salesperson calls me, I know she's taking notes—and good ones—because the next day my order is delivered correctly, or she's back* *with an answer to something I've requested. I can't afford to have a lot of paperwork sitting around on my roll top; I have to know I can go ahead and process the order. With her, I know I can and that's a result of her ability to stay on top of the job."*

Key points from customer interviews

- **Keeping customers is cost-effective.** Don't walk away from a sale after the goods have been delivered. For the customer, that's when the sale really begins. Studies show that it is three to five times cheaper to keep a customer than to acquire a new one. And satisfied customers are the most likely to be repeat buyers or to buy new products from the company. How do you create satisfied customers? Follow up and follow through.

   If you dine at a fine restaurant, you'll notice that soon after you're served your meal, a waiter will come over and ask, "Is everything all right?" He'll probably return one or two more times with the same question. At the end of the meal, he'll turn up, without your having to call him over, to ask, "More coffee?" Such a waiter is actually a salesperson for this establishment. He knows that he can't just put your food on the table and leave; people return not only for the food, but for the service.

- **Satisfied customers stay loyal.** It's the same in any industry. Your job as a salesperson isn't over when the "food" is delivered. It's also part of your job to determine that the customer is 100 percent satisfied with both the product and the service.

Satisfied customers develop loyalty to your product, service and/or company because they *know that you care* about them. Look at the figures below, compiled by the Rockefeller Institute:

Why customers leave

68%	Feel you don't care
14%	Dissatisfied with product or service
9%	Competitive reasons
3%	Move
1%	Die

- **Back up your customer's decision to buy.** Customers want reassurance that they have made the right decision. Effective follow-through not only gives customers the assurance they need but keeps them coming back for more.

Presumptuousness

Many customers were offended when salespeople asked for their competitors' quotes or put down the competition.

Customer interview: *"If I tell a salesperson that a competitor has quoted me lower rates, I expect him to believe me. If he asks to see the quotes, it's almost as if he's calling me a liar. Why would I do business with him after that?"*

Customer interview: *"Some salespeople are quick to degrade the competition, to tell us what they do wrong. No matter how bad that company is, don't be negative about them. Sometimes I buy from them, too. The minute you knock them down, you're down. You're finished. It's something you have to be very careful about."*

Key points from customer interviews

- **Respect the rules of negotiation.** Customers today are a lot more sophisticated than they used to be. Many have studied the art of negotiation. When they say a competitor has given them a lower price, it may be the truth and it may be a negotiating tactic. It's your job to be a smart negotiator, too. If you argue that the competitor's price couldn't possibly be that low, you lose no matter what. You have to show the customer why your product or service has added value that makes up for the higher price. As one customer said, "There are greater considerations than price. One large factor in making our decision is confidence in the ability to deliver the product as specified in a high-quality, timely manner. I don't want to get calls from the factory saying we can't get this product so we're going to shut down the line. The keys are reliability and availability—they have to be balanced with price."

- **Watch what you say about the competition.** Another thing that frequently turns customers off is when a sales rep talks down the competition. When this happens the customer begins to think, "Why is this rep getting so defensive? If his product is better than the competition, why does he have to put them down?" Or the customer may purchase from more than one vendor, including your competition. In that case, you're casting doubts on his ability to make good choices.

- **Focus on your strengths, not the competitor's weaknesses.** There are times when you may be asked about the competition. For instance, a customer may say, "We use XYZ Company. Why should we switch to you?" Or even, "We're looking at a number of vendors. Right now it's between you and XYZ Company." If you belittle XYZ Company, it will probably put the customer in their corner. A better tactic is to say, "I've heard some good things about that company. But what I want to focus on is how we're different. What we can offer is..." The message you send to the customer is that you are confident and secure, that you believe so strongly in your product or service it's not necessary to tear others down. That's a more realistic—and credible—approach than trying to convince the customer that you're terrific and everyone else in the world is inferior.

"Walk-ins"

Customers' complaints were not so much that people called on them without appointments (although most preferred salespeople not just "pop in"), but that people called without a reason. They also complained about telemarketers who interrupted their day with unwanted phone calls and poor selling skills.

Customer interview: *"I'm a professional. I expect the reps I work with to be professional, too. That means respecting my time. Sometimes I think sales reps say to themselves, 'If I just catch her off guard, she'll do business with me.' That's not the way it works. If you interrupt my day, and then have nothing special to say, it tells me you don't respect me or my business."*

Customer interview: *"People call me on the phone all the time and act as though they're a long lost friend, when I know they're faking. I'd rather they just say, 'Hi. I'm a salesperson. Got a minute while I try to sell you something?' "*

Key points from customer interviews

- **Go back to the basics of common courtesy.** Just because customers say they don't like walk-ins doesn't mean you can never make cold calls. Some of the best sales have been made just walking in off the street. But a little courtesy goes a long way. You must have a clear purpose in mind, a reason a customer should take time out of a busy schedule to see you. This is not the time to ramble on about yourself and your wonderful widgets. If possible, establish a time for you to come back and continue the selling process when the customer is not so busy.

- **Limit your small talk while telemarketing.** When you walk into someone's business or office, you get an immediate sense of how receptive that person is to your call. You can tell if a customer is overwhelmed or exceedingly busy. When you are telemarketing, you have none of these clues to guide you. You may be interrupting a client in the middle of a crisis. Jay Goltz appreciates it when telemarketers get right to the point. "I get calls three times a week from people who start out with, 'Hi, Mr. Goltz, how are you today?'" he says. "The only people who say that to me are people who are trying to sell me something. My friends, my customers, my business associates, they don't say that to me. They might as well say, 'I'm going to pretend to be nice and then sell you something.' I'd much rather have someone say, 'Hi, Mr. Goltz. I know you're busy, but I just wanted to tell you I'm from XYZ Company, and we've got a program to offer you we've found has been very helpful to businesses like yours.' "

- **Be creative and innovative.** Goltz adds that he has the most respect for salespeople who get out of the rut of standard lines that people have been using for years. He wants reps to be direct and up front. "I'd love for someone to call me and say, 'I like what I see in your company. I really want to do business with you, and I'm going to work hard to get you a great price on this.' That would make me feel good. Instead of feeling like the 'victim' of a salesperson, that would make me want to help him out. I respect someone who comes in and tries something different."

"Gabbers"

If a salesperson is talking, that means he or she is not listening and learning. Some salespeople go on and on, thinking they're being friendly. But customers view compulsive talkers as boring time-wasters.

Customer interview: *"There was one rep who used to call me all the time 'just to say hello.' His 'hello' lasted 20 minutes. I couldn't get him off the phone. Supposedly he was calling to find out if I needed anything, but he was doing all the talking."*

Customer interview: *"The best sales rep I work with has the 'gift of listening' rather than the 'gift of gab.' She's very funny, also. I enjoy doing business with her because she knows when it's time to joke around and* *when it's time to get down to business. Some sales reps can't tell the difference."*

Key points from customer interviews

- **Use humor to diffuse difficult situations— when appropriate.** Customers are human; they like to laugh and joke just like everyone else. But being a good storyteller does not necessarily make you a good salesperson. If you're not taking the customer's time seriously, you can easily turn him off. You may think you're creating rapport and bonding, while the customer thinks you're wasting his time. What it really means is you're not spending enough time listening. For more on listening skills, see pages 100-103.

Problem avoiders

Some salespeople would rather do anything than face a customer who is in a crisis. But most customers are more concerned about trying to find solutions to problems than trying to place blame on the rep.

Customer interview: *"Salespeople need to be honest and straightforward...and not withhold information. There have been times in the past where information has been withheld because it wasn't what we wanted to hear. But I'd prefer to hear it. The worst is when someone says, 'We'll deliver it next week' and each week that goes by, they say, 'next week' again. I don't want to be handled that way. Let me know up front so that I can make some other adjustments."*

Customer interview: *"If someone tells me I'm going to have something on Thursday, I shouldn't have to call them on Friday to find out it's not going to be here for another week. I've already committed to installing it on Friday. I don't like to hear bad news, but I'd rather hear it now than find out about it later when I've put my foot in my mouth. When a rep doesn't come through, my credibility suffers and I look bad to my customers."*

Key points from customer interviews

- **Ignoring problems doesn't make them go away.** Customers don't expect you to be perfect, but they do expect you to be honest with them. There are some salespeople who try their best to make problems disappear by simply ignoring them. Of course, that doesn't work. If you don't return a customer's call because you're afraid to face a problem, two things happen: 1) The problem gets out of hand, and 2) the customer will never do business with you again.

- **Be a sympathetic listener.** Sometimes all customers want is an ear. They want to get a complaint off their chest, even if they think there's nothing you can do about it. And often, it turns out there is something you can do if both you and the customer are willing to talk it out and think creatively. What customers want more than anything is to know that you are on their side and will do your best for them whether a problem is your fault or theirs.

Lack of personal respect

Customers resent salespeople who go to other people in the company without their knowledge.

Customer interview: *"I don't make all the buying decisions for my company. Most of the time, I have to run things by my boss. A few times, when I said no to a rep for one reason or another, I find out that he's gone directly to my boss. He may even get away with it once. But believe me, it will never happen again. When the circumstances come to light, neither my boss nor I will ever do business with that rep again."*

Key points from customer interviews

- **Practice top-down selling.** Top sales reps are usually those who practice top-down selling: In other words, start the sales process with the head of the company. Call the office of the president.

Even if you don't get to speak to that person, you'll probably get to his or her assistant, who can usually give you invaluable information about the company. Ask the assistant to direct you to the person who handles the purchase of your type of product or service. When the assistant says, "Bob Jones handles that," you can call Bob Jones, say that you've just been speaking with the president's office and they recommended that you speak to him. That can be the most effective way of reaching the decision-maker.

- **Underhanded tactics do not work in the long run.** "I have a buyer," says Jay Goltz, "and I spend a lot of time delegating responsibilities to others so I don't have to do everything. I think it's insulting to my buyer when reps ask her, 'Are you the decision-maker?' It's as if they're saying to her, 'Am I wasting my time talking to you?' Recently a salesperson called trying to sell me ad space. I told him to speak to my buyer about that. When I let my buyer know this rep would be calling her, she said, 'I spoke to that guy last week.' He went over her head to talk to me. Now I'll never speak with him again. What he should have said was, 'I spoke to her last week, but I know you're the major decision-maker and I wanted to speak directly with you.' I could respect that."

One way you can find out the real decision-maker without being insulting is to say, "Is there anyone else you'd recommend speaking with beside yourself who could give me insight into making the best recommendation for your company?" That way, you're not negating their input and you're expressing your concern about the whole business environment.

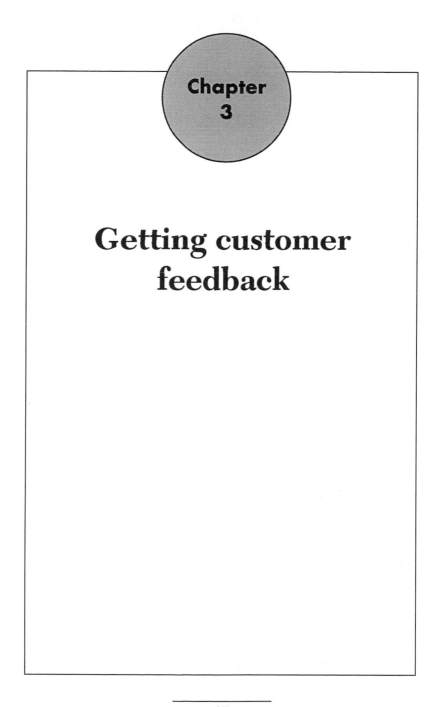

**Chapter
3**

Getting customer
feedback

Sales secrets from your customers

Customers today are more educated than they've ever been before. That means they expect more from salespeople. Recently, studies have been released reporting that customers are less bothered by poor service because they're getting used to it; they're lowering their standards.

I don't believe that's true. I believe that people are as upset as ever about poor quality, bad service and a lack of accountability. However, they don't feel there's much they can do about it.

You can change that perception, not only by giving your customers the best quality and service, but by giving them a voice in setting the high standards they desire—and deserve. *Ask your customers for feedback.* They'll be glad to tell you what you're doing wrong—and what you're doing right. The invaluable information you receive from each of your customers will help you in serving all of your customers.

Telephone surveys

Given the opportunity, most customers are more than willing to give you feedback about how you and your company are doing. One method of getting this feedback is by conducting telephone surveys. It's a worthwhile investment for companies to hire someone to do this;

college students or part-timers can be hired for a modest wage to perform the job.

Develop a questionnaire, with input from all the departments in your company (sales, billing, shipping, customer service, etc.) for feedback on how you can improve in a variety of areas, what you can do to keep your current customers and how you can generate more business with them.

Have the callers ask your customer's permission to tape the conversation. Then at the end of the week, salespeople and management can sit at a table and listen to these interviews with your top customers. Each person in the meeting can then try to find a way to respond to customers' concerns. The customer service department may change the way they answer the phone, sales reps may develop a better system of communication with the shipping department, CEOs may consider developing a line of products that meet more of the customers' needs.

Audiotaping the customer feedback has advantages:

1. Customers are usually more willing to have phone conversations than to fill out a form or write an "essay" about your company's performance.

2. You get to hear exactly what the customer has to say, in full and specific detail.

3. You get to hear the customer's voice inflections. When a customer gets excited, major and minor points become clearer than they ever could on a written survey.

The highlights of these conversations can be transcribed and shown on an overhead projector so that it's easy to follow along.

Some of the questions that can be used in such audio-taped surveys include:

1. Why did you decide to go with our company?
2. Who else did you look at before buying from our company?
3. Who have you worked with in the past that you liked, besides our company?
4. Which of our competitors offers you things that we don't? What are they and how helpful are they to your business?
5. What could our sales reps do to generate more business with you?
6. How can we improve the products or service you currently use in order to help you improve your business?
7. What feedback can you give our front desk or customer service department about how they answer the phone or respond to inquiries?
8. Who was the best sales rep you've ever worked with—from any company—and what did they do to impress you?

Add your own questions or adapt these so that they fit your company or industry. But be careful how you ask questions. Dorothy Leeds, author of *Smart Questions,* says that asking questions in a rote, robotic way will only turn customers off and make them feel uncomfortable. It's important to let the customers know that their responses are important to you, and that you're sincerely interested in what they have to say.

"You also have to probe and clarify to get to the real meaning of customers' answers," says Leeds. "People tend to speak in generalities. If customers say they're unhappy with your service, you need to ask exactly what they're unhappy about. Most reps do that already. But when you ask, 'Are you happy with our service?' you have to probe for the deeper answer, as well. What does it really mean if a customer says, 'Everything's fine'? There are two reasons for probing this answer:

1. Some customers are reluctant to complain. By gently probing about specifics of the service they're receiving, you can usually uncover one or two areas that need improvement.

2. When they do praise your product or service in detail, you can then ask if you may quote them in a testimonial."

Another method of receiving customer feedback is to have your customers call you. Install an 800 number feedback line, where customers can call and either talk to a company representative or leave a recorded message with suggestions on how to improve service. At the end of each week, these comments can also be reviewed and action plans set up based on their feedback.

The customer-run meeting

If you want to know exactly how well—or how poorly—you are performing, there is only one reliable and accurate source for an answer: your customers. Who can better tell you what's expected of you as a sales rep, what's expected of your company and where you fall short of those expectations than customers themselves? Holding six to 15 customer-run meetings a year—in which the customers get free rein in expressing their opinions about your company's performance—you can find out exactly how you need to improve with specific accounts. Just as important, your company will identify recurring service problems that can be resolved to the benefit of all its customers.

The meetings and the resulting improvements can help you maintain customer relations and generate new business, as well. As was said earlier, many customers stop buying because they believe a vendor no longer cares about them or their business. A customer-run meeting shows them you do indeed care about more than racking up sales.

The process of inviting customers in to sit down and have a discussion in your environment allows each customer to get to know you and your organization better, which helps form a closer customer-vendor relationship. It can help your customer become better acquainted with the full line of products and services you offer. You may both discover new ways your two companies can work together. And the information you receive on how to improve your service to this company will likely give you suggestions you can use to improve your service to your other customers, as well.

A good customer-run meeting depends on careful preparation as well as on quick follow-up to a customer's suggestions. The meeting should be led by the person in your company who has the strongest relationship with the customer, whether that's the sales rep who manages the account, the sales manager, etc. The leader's role is to mediate between the customers and your company's participants so that everything goes smoothly. A customer-run meeting creates a win-win-win situation: The customer wins (by getting improved sales and service), the sales rep wins (by learning exactly how this customer wants to be sold) and the company wins (by forging a strong relationship between the three parties). Here are some techniques for facilitating successful customer-run meetings:

- **Select the participants.** Each meeting should be devoted to a *single customer* so that you can focus exclusively on that customer's needs. If other customers participate, each may be reluctant to speak in front of the others. And if they should hear about problems they are not currently experiencing, they may worry that those problems will arise. Invite your largest client first, since losing this client would have the greatest impact on your bottom line. Then you can work your way down to smaller accounts.

  Invite people from several departments at the client company, such as an end user, a purchasing manager and a general/financial manager. That way, you'll get different perspectives on the company's needs. The people attending from your own company should include the salesperson in charge of the account and anyone else you think might benefit, including other reps, service employees and your sales and billing managers.

- **Set an agenda.** The purpose of the meeting is for the customer to discuss any problems he may be having with your company, and to make suggestions on how you might improve. But without structure, the meeting will probably focus more on complaints than on solutions. It's up to the sales manager to set the agenda and make sure the meeting results in at least three or four suggestions on how to strengthen the relationship.

  Remember that this meeting is not a thinly disguised sales pitch. Customers are not there to listen to another sales presentation. Reps should listen carefully and stay focused on finding out how better to meet their customers' needs. It's not unusual, however, for such a meeting to result in additional sales as participants uncover new opportunities to work together.

- **Hold the meeting on-site.** The meeting, and the relationship, become more personal when customers have a visual reference of your work site. They can associate the staff's name with their faces and get a better sense of how your company operates. If possible, take them on a tour of the facilities. Be sure to make the customer aware of any product lines they don't currently buy, as well as any that are in the development stage.

- **Set up and open the meeting.** When the customer walks into the meeting room, participants from your company should be sitting in their places with note pads in front of them. The impression you want to make is that of a room of scientists dedicated to finding the perfect formula for improving service to him and his company. The facilitator should open the meeting by introducing the customer and other participants from his company, and then give a brief rundown of the agenda and the purpose of the meeting.

- **Keep the meeting focused on the customer's input.** Make up a list of questions you want to ask the customer (see page 97). When asking them, however, remember to spend three-fourths of the time listening—not talking. Respond directly to all complaints. Don't be defensive. If a customer says your company waits too long to make service calls, and you've already pegged this as an area for improvement, you can say, "We are already working to solve this problem. But please tell us exactly what has been happening so that we can help you specifically." If a customer complains about an area in which you've had no prior complaints, say, "Please explain this in more detail so we can do something about it." Some customers may be hesitant about voicing negative comments. If that's the case, reassure them by saying, "The only way this meeting will be a success is if you share some problems or concerns you're having so we can remedy them immediately."

Have someone in the room record the customer's comments on a flip chart. This not only shows the customer you value his comments, it makes it easier to summarize the main points at the end of the meeting. Then you can distill these points into four or five actions you will take to improve your relationship with the customer.

- **Explore ways to help the customer meet his own customers' needs.** Often, during your discussions, points will come up that will help the customer be more competitive in his market. One office products company, for example, learned in a customer-run meeting that it needed to implement a computerized sales-tracking system. The customer, a bank, was so satisfied with the results that it purchased a program to help manage its own sales force more effectively. This system had nothing to do with the products the original company was selling, but they were happy to connect the bank with the proper vendor. When something like that happens, the customer will perceive your company as a partner, rather than just another vendor supplying products at a price.

- **Offer attendees a token of appreciation.** Customers have taken time out of their busy schedules to meet with you. A small gift is a nice sign of your appreciation for their help and input. The gifts need not be expensive; a clock, a camera, a plaque, a T-shirt or a pen will do fine. You may even want to offer a personalized gift based on what you know about the customer's interest, such as monogrammed golf tees if he or she plays.

- **Debrief the staff after the meeting.** Go back over the customer's recommendations and assign problem-solving duties to those responsible for each service glitch. Ask your employees whether other customers have been experiencing similar problems. That way, you can use the tips you've gathered to make across-the-board changes that strengthen other relationships.

- **Create a meeting report.** Describe your initial meeting objectives, why the customer was selected and the five or six most important points covered at the meeting. Then, develop an action plan for implementing customer suggestions.

- **Implement the customer's suggestions.** Speed is of the essence when the meeting ends. A customer whose problems are solved, and solved quickly, via customer-run meetings will think more highly of your company than a customer who never had a problem at all. Immediately following the meeting, send the customer a letter outlining the steps you will take to improve service. If you can't make suggested changes, say so in the letter and explain why.

- **Ask your customer questions.** To get honest feedback from a customer, ask direct questions about how you can better serve the customer's needs. Some examples:

  - What are the key characteristics you look for in a successful vendor relationship?

  - What are the major turnoffs to doing business with us that could deteriorate our business relationship?

  - What problems are you having with us or with your business in general?

  - Who are your main customers, and what are you trying to accomplish with them?

  - Who is your competition, and what are you doing to differentiate yourself from them?

  - What are the three most important areas of your business?

  - What are the three most important things we can do as a vendor to keep our relationship strong?

  - What's the best way for a new salesperson to approach you?

  - What does a salesperson do to make a good first impression on you?

- What should a salesperson ask you if he or she wants to know more about your business and needs?

- What have salespeople (from any company) done that really impressed you or made a difference in the sales process?

- If a salesperson thinks he or she has a solution that fits your need but isn't sure whether you have the budget for it, how should he or she find out?

- What do you like best about our company?

- What do you like least about our company?

- What are some of your day-to-day frustrations in doing business with us?

- If you were in our shoes, what would you do differently to service yourself as a customer?

- If you were in charge of our company, what would you do differently?

Customer-run meeting checklist

Pre-meeting

Comments / Responsibilities / Due Dates

Decide on meeting objectives_____

Customer selection_____

Decide on staff attendees_____

Develop questions_____

Develop agenda_____

Select time and place_____

Issue invitation to customer—oral and written_____

Other_____

Meeting

Introduction of attendees_____

Statement of meeting objectives_____

Introductory statement by customer_____

Questions_____

Closing remarks_____

Appreciation of customer_____

*Certificate_____ *Gift_____

Tour, lunch or final activity_____

Other_____

Post-meeting

Debriefing meeting_____

  *What was said?_____

  *What are areas for improvement?_____

Action plan_____

"Thank you" letter to customer_____

Meeting report (one page)_____

Other_____

Improve your listening skills

Listen for information. Information is the key to sales success. Too often, salespeople use the time when the customer is talking to launch their presentation. Learn to distinguish emotional messages from information. Often, when we're nervous, we're thinking about what we're going to say next and we're not really listening at all. This can be a real sales-killer. Concentrate on what the other person is saying. Be sure it makes sense to you. Take notes so you can ask questions later if you need to.

If you listen carefully, your customers will always tell you what they need most from you. Author Lisa Kanarek says, "It's easy to forget to listen to your clients. For months after my book came out, I was getting phone calls and during the course of the conversation, people would ask, 'Do you have an audio version of your book?' After the tenth such conversation, I realized I needed an audio version of my book. If customers are asking you for something, don't just write it off and say 'it can't be done.' Explore the possibilities. Pay attention to what they're telling you."

Some basics for developing the critical skill of listening:

- *Be aware of the customer's body language.* The way a customer moves, shifts, leans forward or back often tells you more than his words. Is he bored, impatient, tired, excited, interested? Top salespeople can translate body language and respond to it, just as they respond to the customer's words. If someone is constantly looking at his watch or looking at the wall with a blank expression, that's a clear hint you're talking too much. It's time to start asking questions, to get them talking. When a customer's talking, he won't be bored unless he's bored with himself.

On the other hand, don't over-analyze every movement or gesture. I once heard that if a person scratches their nose, it means they don't trust you, and if they rub their chin, they're very interested. What the heck does it mean if someone scratches their chin and rubs their nose? Who knows? Better go back to listening to what the customer is saying.

- *Be aware of your own body language.* Your body language tells the customer whether or not you are really interested in him and his problems. Make eye contact. Lean forward in your chair to hear what she says. Listen enthusiastically. That doesn't mean you have to jump up and down at everything the customer says, but do comment occasionally with a "Really?" or an "I understand." Focus on trying to get the core information from that customer. Remember, you're there to learn. Your willingness to listen and learn will earn you big points and make the customer feel important. After all, who doesn't like to be considered interesting?

- *Eliminate distractions.* You may not be able to stop your customer's phone from ringing or control how many times his assistant interrupts your meeting. But you can eliminate your own distractions. Clear your mind of everything except the customer's situation. All your personal and business distractions should be put aside; they will still be waiting for you when you are through with the customer. When you're with a customer, be there for him 100 percent. If you're not paying attention, if you're distracted and unfocused, customers will perceive you to be that way all the time—and won't trust that you'll be there for them when they need you.

- *Don't make judgments or interpretations until you've heard the whole story.* Put yourself in the speaker's shoes and wait for the entire message. Too often salespeople hear a key phrase and they jump to a conclusion and try to close the sale. Compensation is not paid for the speed of the close, just for the close.

- *Don't let your personal opinions cloud your selling skills.* A professional situation is not the arena for settling political or religious differences. It doesn't matter if your customer has a different organizational philosophy. What matters is whether or not your product or service offers the customer an honest solution to his needs or problems. There is good in everyone. If you can hook into that part of the person or organization, then you can find a way to work together. If you can't find that hook, pass this person on to someone else in your company.

- *Avoid expectations.* Some salespeople are so anxious to make a sale they don't really hear what the customer is saying. They try to force-fit what the customer is saying into some preconceived product or service solution. That approach never works. It may be that your product/service doesn't meet the customer's need at all. Trying to force him into a mold will just alienate him and shut off information which might trigger a solution that would work for both of you.

    Don't jump onto something that sounds exciting before you've heard all the information. Salespeople want instant gratification. We want to sell a product right away, and if it's not right, we want to try to make it fit. You want to make sure that you can come up with a solution that's in the customer's best interest. There may be some situations where the customer is better off with what they presently own or with a competitor's product. That customer will respect you for telling the truth and will become your loyal supporter.

- *Be sure you understand what customer mean, not just what they say.* Customers have the same communication problems we all do; we mean to say one thing and we say another. Unless you check what you hear, you will not know if you heard and understood correctly. There was one large account I was working on where it took me a long time to get into the account, and I was developing a relationship with a buyer there. During one conversation, we were exchanging information about our personal lives. The buyer said to me, "I'm having twins." I thought he said, "I *had* twins." So I said, "Really? Two boys? A boy and a girl?" He answered, "Well, one's a boy, but we're not quite sure about the other one." Thinking this was a very bizarre answer, I stared at him as if he had seven heads. In the back of my mind I was saying to myself, "Maybe this guy needs a second opinion from another doctor!" Seeing the strange look I was giving him, he gave me an even stranger one. I decided the best thing to do was to change the subject, and quickly got back to business.

A few weeks later I called his office and his assistant told me he was at the hospital, and that his wife had just given birth to twins. At that point, I realized my mistake. The buyer's answer suddenly made sense. When I finally saw the buyer again, I reminded him of our strange conversation and he told me, "No wonder you had that strange look on your face!" He had a good laugh about it. I had every intent of listening carefully during our conversation. Simply by missing a few letters in one word, I got the story all wrong. So be sure to double-check everything a customer tells you, especially if it sounds a little strange.

- *Boost your memory.* Confucius once said, "Short pencil better than long memory." Take notes and use those notes to check your understanding of what was said. These notes will also help when you call back. You can start a conversation with, "When we were last together, you said..." and make an impression on the customer that you were really listening.

"Magic questions"

The following list of "magic questions" was developed by Sandy Erickson, National Sales Trainer for Val-Pak. Sandy developed these questions when she was running her own Val-Pak franchise. She found that these questions elicited information other questions didn't normally get. She was playing the role of detective, trying to get as many clues as possible in order to solve her customers' problems. What makes a great detective great is what he asks himself, not what he tells himself. And what makes a great salesperson great is what he asks his customers, not what he tells them.

The questions are used by Val-Pak reps to understand a retailer's customers. These questions were, of course, developed for Sandy Erickson's particular situation, but you can adapt this series of questions to fit your company and industry. After you ask each of these questions, let the buyer talk while you listen and take notes.

- "Before we get down to business, I'm just curious, how did you get into this business?" Buyer talks, salesperson listens. This leads to learning about the buyer's expertise and goals.

- "How long has this business been here?" This leads to learning about the company's position in the market.

- "How have things changed since _____?" This leads to uncovering current marketing problems to formulate the ad mission.

- "What is a typical customer like?" This leads to identifying the target consumer.

- "What is the most popular item you sell?" This leads to formulation of good offers and realistic expectations.

- "How much, on the average, does your customer spend?" This leads to formulation of good offers and realistic expectations.

- "Where else can they buy these products?" This identifies the competitive position in the market and its effect on the mission of the advertising.

- "If you met someone for the first time, what would you say about your business to make them want to buy from you?" This leads to a summary of the message that needs to be delivered.

If the buyer is reticent, skip to the last question. Buyers have generally thought long and hard about the subject and have plenty to say about it.

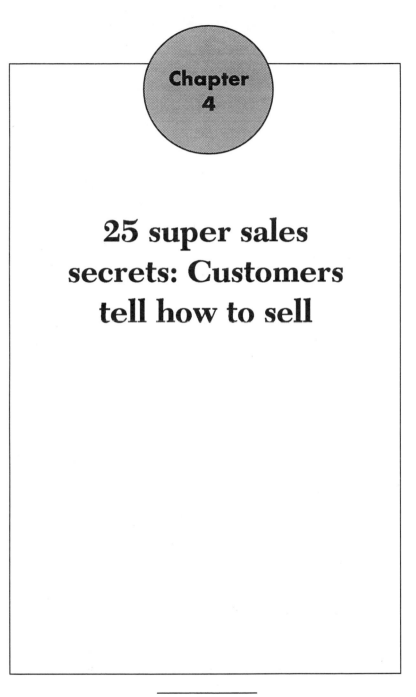

Chapter 4

25 super sales secrets: Customers tell how to sell

One of the things I found most interesting about conducting customer interviews was just how willing the customers were to share their opinions and insights. In fact, in many instances, I couldn't shut them up. That told me two things:

1. They felt the points they were making were of extreme importance, and they appreciated being asked.
2. Most of them had not been asked before.

Our customers are a rich asset, waiting to be mined. It's a shame to waste such a valuable resource. Every company should be asking not "What can we sell you?" but "How are we doing?" and "What can we do better?"

25 super sales secrets

Our customers have the secrets of how to sell to them. Here are just some of the ones they've shared with me:

1. Don't sell me your product—sell me solutions.
2. Understand my business, understand my industry and understand my market.
3. Understand your product or service thoroughly so that you know every conceivable way it

might help me solve my problems or meet my goal.

4. Know everything you can about your competition. I have to make decisions about which product is best, and I need to know what makes yours the best choice for me.

5. Watch what you say about the competition. I want to know why your product is the best choice, but I don't want you to knock the competition. Concentrate on your strengths, not their weaknesses.

6. Don't give me a canned, generic pitch. Appreciate my unique qualities and challenges.

7. Have my best interest at heart.

8. Make me feel important. Make me believe I'm the only customer you have—even though I know it's not true.

9. Have a purpose for every call.

10. Organize your materials so that when I ask to see information, you have it easily accessible.

11. Return my calls promptly. I expect that you'll be as available to talk to me now as you were before the sale was completed.

12. Let me know how to reach you. If I can't find you, I'll go with someone else.

13. Help me solve a problem, even if it's your fault, and I'll most likely remain a loyal customer.

14. I'm looking for a sales rep I can consider a member of my team, a partner—almost an employee. When you help me find solutions to run my business better, it's easier for me to see you in that light.

15. Keep your promises. If you say you'll get back to me, do it.

16. Anyone can make a one-time sale. It's the follow-through that keeps me coming back for more.

17. If you don't have an immediate answer, don't try to fake it or make one up. I'd rather you say, "I don't know, but I'll find out." Of course, once you say that, you must get back to me with the answer as soon as possible.

18. Let me know that you're interested in my success. If that means that you sometimes recommend the competition or tell me I'm better off with the product or service I now have, I'll respect you greatly and find a way to do business with you in the future.

19. Be my consultant. Show me how others in my field have been successful. Become a resource for me so that I can call on you when I'm in a bind and need advice—even if it's got nothing to do with your product or service.

20. Create added value. Price is not my only criterion. The extra service and special attention you give me is worth more than dollars in many instances.

21. Exceed my expectations. Let me know that you are willing to go beyond the norm, to make that extra effort it takes to ensure success—mine and yours.

22. Don't keep me waiting. If you're going to be late, call me.

---

23. Exhibit a positive attitude and enthusiasm about your job and your product. If you don't believe in yourself, I won't believe in you either.

24. Don't argue with me or be too aggressive. If I feel like I'm being pushed into a sale, I know you're interested in your commissions, not your customers.

25. Be honest with me in all situations. If there are problems, let me know so that together we can begin to think of solutions.

Chapter 5

Customer service questionnaire: 40 questions to ask yourself

Successful salespeople are always surveying their customers to find out how they're doing. But it's just as important to survey yourself, to keep yourself on track and in line with the kinds of comments customers made throughout this book. Once a month, go over this list of questions. Answer them honestly, and you'll know whether you're meeting your customers' needs and desires.

40 questions to ask yourself

1. Do I treat everyone I know and meet with respect and courtesy because they might be my next customer?

2. When I am a customer myself, do I observe and learn from the salesperson's strengths and weaknesses?

3. Do I have a thorough knowledge of my product or service?

4. Do I have a thorough knowledge of my customer's product, company and industry?

5. Do I have a thorough knowledge of my competitors' strengths and weaknesses?

6. Do I read newsletters and trade publications from my customers' industries?

7. Do I understand my customer's target market? Can I make suggestions to help him reach that market?

8. Have I talked to customers who have used my product for a while so that I can get an end-user's point of view?

9. Do I let my customers know that I understand their uniqueness and their individual goals and challenges?

10. Do I truly empathize with each client's needs and problems?

11. Do I ask questions that will help me understand the other person's position?

12. Do the rest of the people in the company know what the customer's needs are (the service department, the billing department, etc.)?

13. Do I make each customer feel important?

14. Am I prepared for every call I make?

15. Do I have a good reason for every call I make?

16. Have I asked myself the three important pre-call questions:

    What is the goal of the call?

    What do I need to find out during the call?

    What's the next step after this call?

17. Have I studied each customer's style? Do I know who likes to chat and schmooze and who likes to get right down to business?

18. Are all of my presentations clear, concise and organized?

19. Do I return my customers' calls as soon as I can, even if I know there's a problem involved?

20. Do my customers know how to reach me whenever they need to?

21. Do I ever make promises I know I can't keep?

22. Do I have an organized system of follow-up?

23. Do I send thank-you notes even when I don't get the business?

24. What tools do I use for follow-up besides the telephone?

25. If a customer leaves, do I know why?

26. If I don't know why, do I ask?

27. Do I ask every customer I have, "Is there anything I'm not doing that I should be doing?"

28. Do I listen 70 percent of the time?

29. Do I consider myself a resource for my customers—even in areas not associated with my business?

30. Do I create added value for my customers by going beyond what's expected?

31. Do I look for ways to help my customers increase their bottom lines?

32. Do I treat my time—and my customers' time—as a precious commodity?

33. Do I prioritize my activities so that what must get done does get done?

34. Do I put in 110 percent effort all the time?

35. After every task, do I ask myself, "Can I do it better?"

36. Do I greet my customers with a positive attitude, energy and enthusiasm?

37. Am I honest with my customers, even when I have to tell them bad news?

38. Do I know the difference between aggressiveness and assertiveness?

39. Do I respect my customers' ideas, opinions and right to object? Am I patient and willing to answer questions without arguing?

40. Do I try to find creative, innovative ways to approach new customers—and keep the ones I have?

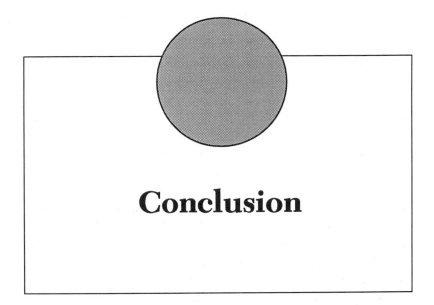

Conclusion

Picture this scene: You're at a neighborhood restaurant. There is no atmosphere to speak of, although the place is neat and clean. The food is edible, nothing more. The prices are the same as most of the other eateries around. Yet people are standing on line in the rain waiting to get in. Why? Because the owner, who stands at the door every night, recognizes his customers, knows their names and their family histories. The waitress is funny and pleasant and comes to refill your coffee without being asked. And when the chef peeks out and sees your familiar face in the room, he decides to send over a free dessert to show his appreciation for your patronage. In decor, atmosphere and even food, this restaurant is mediocre. But its customers return again and again, because they know they can *count on the service.*

That's the foundation for what every customer interviewed for this book had to say: "Let me know I can count on you to be there for me. Show me by your actions that you value my business and respect me as a human being. Make me feel important." Basic? Perhaps. But it's what we need to go back to time and time again to remind ourselves who we serve and how we can serve them better. Because, of course, it will all come back to us in the end. If you give people more than they expect, it causes them to react in a positive manner. You make them want to give back to you—with new business, with referrals, with testimonials.

Remember this: When a successful sales rep leaves and goes to a competitor, his customers usually follow. They're more loyal to the person who extended them extra service, who was interested in their success, who helped them out in times of need. Isn't that how you'd like your customers to think of you?

I'd be happy to hear from you with any comments or ideas you'd like to share. Write to me at:

Farber Training Systems
250 Ridgedale Avenue
Suite Q5
Florham Park, NJ 07932

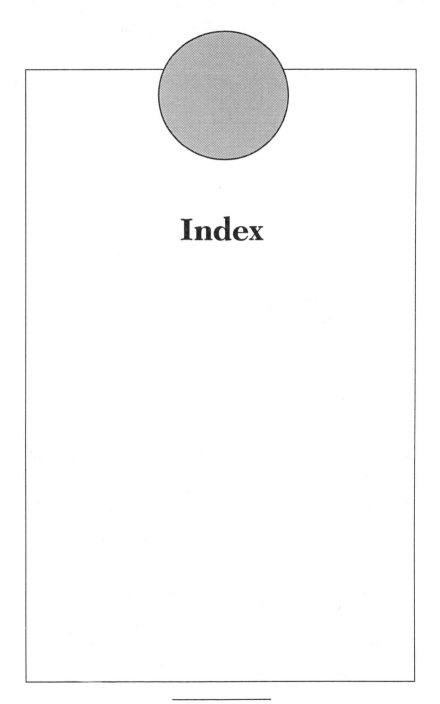

Index